OUTSIDE AND INSIDE
SNAKES

BY

SANDRA MARKLE

Atheneum Books for Young Readers

Cat-eyed snake eating a frog's eggs

For Corliss Evans, with great admiration

The author would especially like to thank the following for sharing their enthusiasm and expertise: Dr. Harry W. Greene, curator of herpetology and professor of integrative biology, University of California, Berkeley, California; Dr. L. A. Wilson, Fernbank Science Center, Atlanta, Georgia; Dr. Gordon W. Schuett, postdoctoral research associate, Arizona State University West, Phoenix, Arizona; and Laura White Schuett.

READERS' NOTE: To help readers pronounce words that may not be familiar to them, there is a pronunciation guide on page 37. These words are italicized the first time they appear.

Atheneum Books for Young Readers
An imprint of Simon & Schuster Children's Book Publishing Division
1230 Avenue of the Americas
New York, New York 10020

The text of this book is set in 16-point Melior.
Typography by Christy Hale
Printed in Hong Kong
10   9   8   7   6   5

Library of Congress Cataloging-in-Publication Data

Markle, Sandra.
    Outside and inside snakes / by Sandra Markle.
        p.   cm.
    ISBN 0-02-762315-7
        1. Snakes—Juvenile literature. [1. Snakes.]   I. Title.
QL666.06M257   1995
    597.966—dc20   94-20647
Summary: Discusses snakes' diet, locomotion, reproduction, respiration, etc.

Snakes are amazing! They can move without any arms or legs. Some even swim and climb tall trees. How do they do that? And how do they catch their food? Would you believe a snake can swallow food that is larger than its head! For you, that would be like swallowing a big melon—whole. Why does a snake flick its tongue in and out so often? And why does a snake never blink? This book will let you find out all these things and more. You'll even take a peek inside a snake.

This is a yellow eyelash viper.
To see it in action, turn the page!

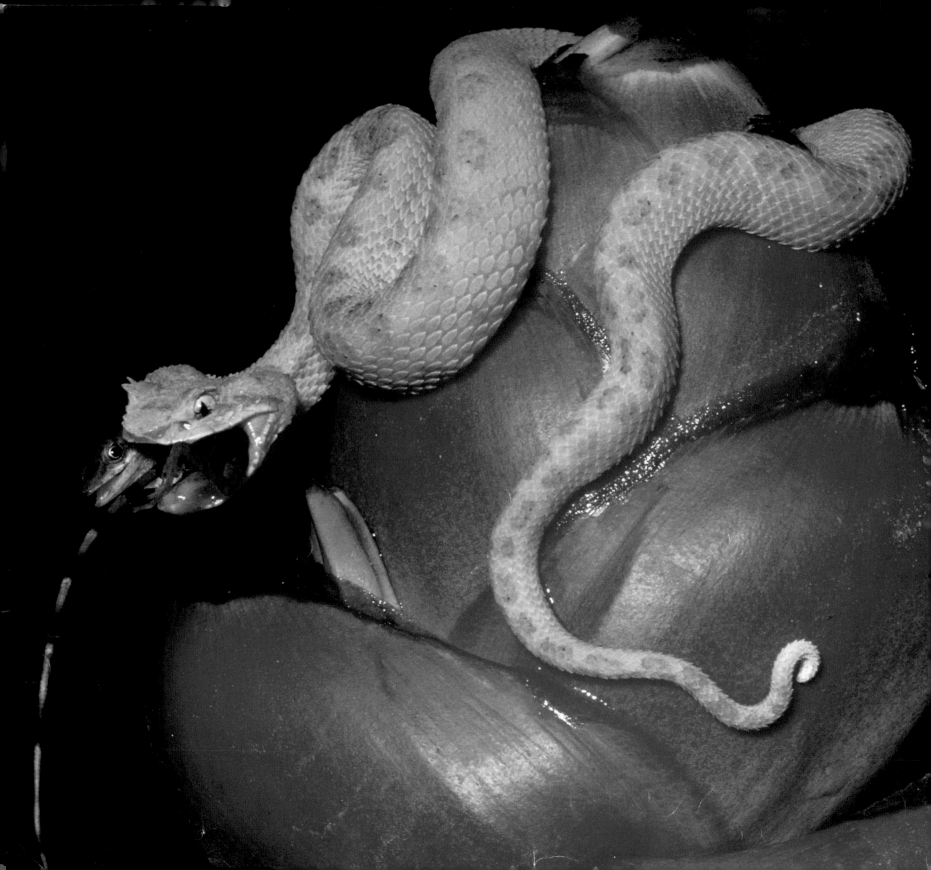

Did you think this was a snake? It's really a snake lizard. If you watched it long enough, the snake lizard would blink. Most lizards have eyelids. Snakes do not, so a snake cannot blink. A snake's eyes are covered by clear scales.

The bright yellow eyelash viper just caught a lizard. Not having arms or legs did not keep it from catching its dinner. In fact, a snake's long shape and strong body help it find food. This snake was able to climb and hang on while it waited to catch something to eat. Snakes that go looking for food are helped by their shape, too. They can move easily through thick grass and small openings.

A snake's shape also helps it stay safe. Enemies may not notice a snake coiled up and hiding under leaves or stretched out along a tree limb. The snake might even escape by slipping into a space too small for its enemy to follow.

After this python lies on the sunny rock ledge for a while, its body temperature will likely be about the same as yours. Usually, though, a snake's temperature is lower than yours. So if you touch a snake, it will feel cool.

Snakes spend a lot of time doing nothing—or so it seems. Lying around is really very important for a snake. Like you, a snake has to be warm to be active and to digest its food. Your body produces the heat it needs from the food you eat. But a snake changes its food into energy too slowly to provide the heat it needs. That is why a snake has to spend time soaking up heat from the warm ground or air. It also means a snake does not need to eat as often as you do.

African bush viper

Emerald tree boa

Imagine how scratchy it would feel to crawl across rocks, sand, or tree bark. A snake's body is protected by a tough body suit of plates and scales that is just its body size. This coat is nearly watertight, too. It keeps in body water, which is very important for snakes living in deserts. It also sheds water outside the snake's body, like a raincoat. So if you touch a snake, it will feel dry.

Look closely at the scales of the two snakes in the pictures. Some snakes, like the bush viper, have scales with a ridge down the middle. Others, like this tree boa, have smooth scales. In some cases, the pattern of a snake's scales can be used to tell what kind of snake it is.

See the folds of skin around the snake's mouth? These help it grip the egg while swallowing.

Were you surprised this African egg-eating snake could stretch enough to swallow such a big egg? One reason it could is that its scales are spots of thicker skin folded over thinner, stretchy skin. As the egg moves into the snake's tube-shaped body, the skin unfolds.

By bending its neck, this snake pushes the egg against sharp bones, breaking the shell. Then the snake spits out the shell. Most other kinds of egg-eating snakes are able to digest eggs shell and all.

See this black rat snake's wide belly scales? The edges of these scales press against any rough spots on the tree's bark, helping the snake keep a good grip as it moves from branch to branch.

How can you tell where a snake's body stops and the tail starts? One big belly scale, the anal scale, marks the end of the body. An opening under this scale is where the snake's wastes come out.

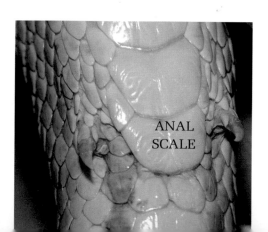

ANAL SCALE

10

Is this a bright yellow worm or the snake's tail?

Did you guess that what looks like a yellow worm is the snake's tail? Like most other snakes, this cantil is colored to blend in and hide—except for its tail. Any lizard or frog that tries to catch the "worm" may become the snake's dinner.

Now take a close look at the adder hiding in the desert sand. How did its skin coloring help it catch the lizard? Why do you suppose the adder's eyes are on top of its head?

A snake's skin is really made up of several layers of cells stacked one on top of the other. Cells are like tiny building blocks. The cells forming the outer portion of the skin are dead. This outer skin shields the living cells underneath.

Soon the tough, dead outer portion of the skin shown in the picture will be shed. Below the outer portion, special cells have made new inner layers of cells. These deeper cells will form the snake's body surface after the outer layer sheds. They contain the coloring matter that give the snake its special shade and pattern.

A computer combined two different enlarged views to show what a snake's skin looks like six to eight days before shedding.

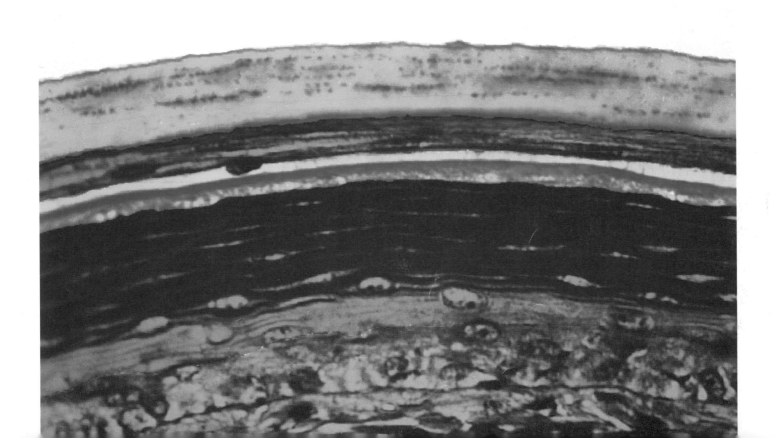

What looks like a hat is this black racer's old skin starting to peel off. Crawling around is hard on a snake's skin, so the snake sheds the outer layer a few times each year. Shedding lets the snake grow bigger and have a body suit that is just right for its new size.

When it's time for a snake to shed, the outer layer of dead cells separates from the living cells underneath. This covering of loose old skin makes the snake's colors look dull. The snake rubs the sides of its mouth against anything rough. When the old skin breaks, the snake tries to catch the loose skin on twigs or rough stones. The old skin comes off, usually in one piece. It peels off inside out, just the way you might take off a sock.

So what's under a snake's skin? Bones, for one thing.

A building has a strong framework to support it and give it shape. A snake's body, like yours, has a framework—a bony *skeleton*.* But a snake's skeleton is very different from yours. For one thing, you have arms and legs. A snake does not. You also have only thirty-three backbones and twenty-four ribs. A long snake may have more than three hundred backbones, or *vertebrae*, with a pair of ribs attached to all backbones but those of the neck and tail.

Do you wonder why a snake's skeleton has so many backbones? Its body, like yours, can only bend where two bones meet. Having lots of small bones lets it coil and bend easily.

* See page 37 to help you pronounce words that are *italicized* the first time they appear.

Muscles, body parts that pull on bones, hook a snake's ribs to its belly scales. So when the muscles pull on the ribs, they move these scales, too.

One set of muscles raises the scales and moves them forward. Another set of muscles lowers the scales and pushes them backward. The lower edge of the snake's belly scales are not attached to its body. So as these scales move backward, they dig into the surface underneath the snake. Did you ever shove your feet against the side of a swimming pool to glide forward? The backward push by the belly scales works the same way to move the snake forward. Why do you think the snake in this picture is having an easier time moving over sand than it would over a slick surface, like glass?

What do you think will happen next?

Did you guess that the yellow eyelash viper would try to catch the bird? Look back at the picture of this snake coiled and waiting, on page 17. Its body is wrapped around the plant, with the front part forming a loose S-shape. As soon as the hummingbird came close enough, the eyelash viper straightened its neck, thrusting its head forward. At the same instant, it opened its mouth wide, so it was ready to bite the bird.

A snake depends on its senses to find food and to stay safe. Males also use their senses to find a mate. Some snakes that hunt by sight, like this parrot snake, have big eyes. Like most daytime hunters, the parrot snake has round pupils. The pupil is an opening that lets light enter the eye. Most nighttime hunters, like the hognose viper on page 24, have oval pupils. This pupil closes to a slit in bright light. At night, the oval pupil opens wide to let in as much light as possible.

A few kinds of snakes, like this rattlesnake, have a sense that helps them hunt even when it is very dark. See the two dark spots just above the snake's mouth? They contain cells that let the snake sense differences in temperature—even very tiny differences. So the snake can "spot" an animal because it is a different temperature than its surroundings. The snake can also judge how far away the animal is. And it can do this quickly enough to strike before the animal gets away.

COMPUTER COLOR-ENHANCED

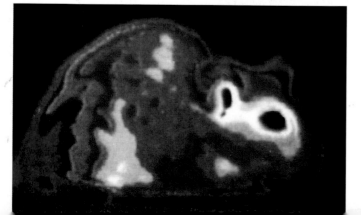

This picture of a mouse was taken using special heat-sensitive film. Warmer parts of the mouse are a different color than cooler parts.

A snake does not have to open its mouth to stick out its tongue. There is a small notch between its upper and lower jaws to let the tongue flick in and out. Why do you think this snake is sticking out its tongue?

You might be surprised to learn that the snake is flicking its tongue in and out to smell the air. Snakes can smell with their noses, but smell is such an important sense to snakes that just breathing in odors is not enough. A snake's moist tongue collects tiny bits of scent matter from the air and from anything it touches. When the tongue is pulled back into the mouth, the tips brush against small bumps on the floor of the mouth. Muscles push the scent-coated bumps up to a pair of pits on the roof of the mouth. The liquid in the snake's mouth carries the scent matter to groups of scent-sensitive cells. These cells send out messages to the brain. Almost instantly the brain processes these messages, and the snake becomes aware of the "smell."

COMPUTER COLOR-ENHANCED

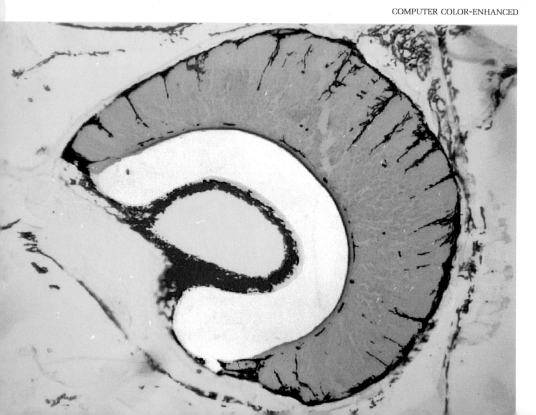

This is one of the pair of scent-sensitive pits in the roof of a garter snake's mouth.

This tropical milk snake has caught a mouse. Since mice eat crops, farmers find these snakes helpful.

All snakes are hunters. None eat vegetables or fruit. But they only have their body and their teeth to catch food. Small, harmless animals or ones that are easy to catch, such as worms or tadpoles, may just be gulped down. Then they are killed inside the snake's stomach by the lack of *oxygen,* a gas in the air they need to live. But bigger, stronger animals can fight back. So some snakes, like this tropical milk snake, coil their bodies around their prey. Then they slowly tighten their hold until the animal stops struggling.

Other snakes use their sharp teeth, or fangs, to catch their food. And some snakes have another weapon—*venom*. Venom is a liquid poison made in a sac-like body part behind the snake's eye. Do you see the hognose viper's fangs stuck in the frog's back? This bite injects some of the snake's venom. Then the snake usually holds on until the frog stops moving.

A snake that uses its venom to catch big, strong animals may bite and then let go. This keeps the snake from being hurt while the animal struggles. Within several minutes, the venom takes effect and the animal drops in its tracks. Then the snake follows the animal's scent trail to its meal.

The yellow drop is venom. Hold a piece of cracker in your mouth, and you will soon feel it soften and crumble. A snake's venom acts like this, beginning to break up food even before the snake swallows.

A snake can really open wide to swallow its food. It can do that because the muscles and tendons that hold its upper and lower jawbones together are stretchy. Now look at the skull. Find the bone between the snake's upper and lower jaws. This bone helps a snake hold its mouth wide open.

Now imagine moving the right side of your lower jaw without moving the left. You cannot do this because the two halves of your lower jaw are hooked together in the front. The two sides of a snake's lower jawbone are separate, but they are held loosely together by muscles. To pull the frog into its mouth, the hognose viper tugs first with half of its lower jaw and then with the other half. Next it jerks its upper jaw forward. Then it "walks" each side of its lower jaw forward again. By doing this over and over, the snake slowly swallows the frog. Digestive juices, like saliva, given off inside the snake's mouth help the frog slip down its throat.

A snake's teeth are all sharp—good for gripping food, but not for chewing. So a snake always swallows its food whole.

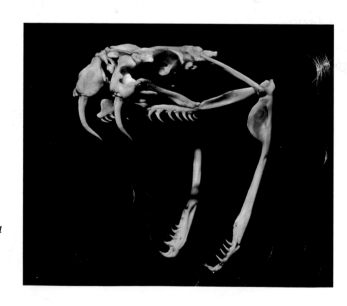

What looks like a tube inside the snake's mouth is its windpipe. It may take the snake more than an hour to swallow something big. So it pushes the end of its windpipe forward and breathes through it while its throat is blocked.

Wonder how a snake's tube-shaped body can stretch around a big meal? Slide your hand down the middle of your chest. You can feel the breastbone that joins your ribs. A snake's ribs do not join, and so they can spread wide apart.

Once the food is swallowed, it goes into the stomach. There pressure from squeezing muscles and special juices start to break down the food—even the bones. When the food is a pulpy mass, the stomach's muscles push it into the small intestine. Now more juices finish breaking down the food into the five basic food *nutrients—proteins, carbohydrates*, fats, minerals, and vitamins. The snake's body will use these to grow and be healthy. The nutrients pass through the walls of the small intestine and into the blood. Then the blood carries them to all parts of the snake's body.

COLOR-ENHANCED

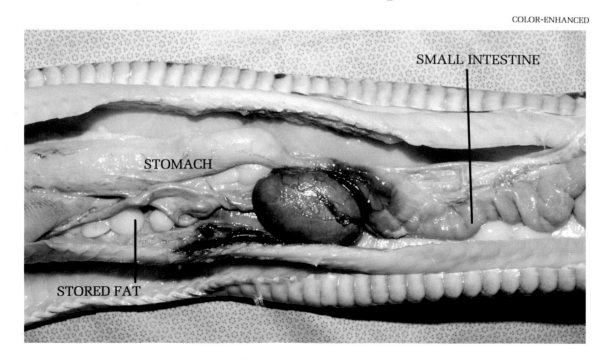

SMALL INTESTINE

STOMACH

STORED FAT

In sea snakes, a special body part under the snake's tongue collects salt from the seawater it drinks. Then the snake pushes out the salt by pushing out its tongue.

You eat several times a day, but a snake usually eats only once every couple of weeks, or even less often. So a snake's body stores fat and breaks down this food as needed.

Wastes are collected in the large intestine. There water in the wastes is returned to the body. Body parts called kidneys also collect wastes from the blood flowing through them. And they recycle more water. Recycling water is especially important to desert snakes.

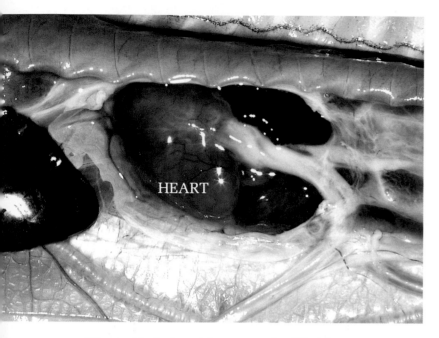

HEART

The snake's heart is a muscle. Blood flows into the darker-colored parts and is pushed out and through the body by the lighter-colored part.

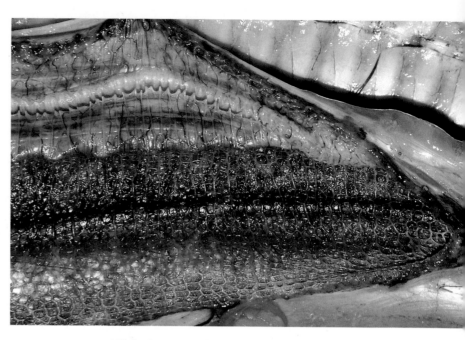

This is part of a snake's lung. The many tiny bubble-like spots are where oxygen enters the blood and carbon dioxide moves into the lung to be breathed out.

    A snake breathes in when muscles lift its ribs, making its body a bigger tube. The lung expands inside this bigger space and air is sucked in to fill it. Air flows through the lung like water through a sponge. As it does, oxygen passes into the blood. Then the heart beats, pushing the blood throughout the snake's body. The snake's body cells combine oxygen with food nutrients to give off energy. And this energy lets the snake be active and grow. In the process, *carbon dioxide,* a waste gas, is given off. It is carried by the blood to the lung. The snake breathes out when its muscles relax, the ribs lower, and the body wall presses in.

Sometimes a snake's surroundings become too hot, too cold, or too dry. Then the snake survives by finding shelter and becoming inactive. The snake's heartbeat slows much more than when it is asleep, and so do its oxygen and energy needs. Snakes escaping cold winter temperatures seek shelter in caves, holes in the ground, or cracks in rocks. Air does not get as cold under a blanket of soil and rock as it does at the surface.

In some parts of Canada, large groups of garter snakes spend the winter together.

These two male prairie rattlesnakes are fighting, but they will not hurt each other. They twine together and rear up. Then one pushes the other to the ground. They do this again and again until one gives up. Although experts disagree about why male rattlers do this, most think it is to win a chance to mate with a female.

In places where it is warm and there is lots of food, females usually produce young once a year. Many kinds of snakes, though, have young only every two or three years. Producing young takes a lot of the female snake's energy.

When snakes mate, a cell from the male called a sperm joins with the female's egg. Then cells at one spot on the egg divide and form the *embryo,* or young. The rest of the egg is the yolk, supplying food for the growing embryo.

In some snakes, the eggs leave the mother's body just as the embryo is starting to develop. So the egg has a tough shell to protect the baby inside. But the shell is also stretchy, so it can expand as the embryo grows. Tiny holes in the shell let water and oxygen in and carbon dioxide out.

The red tubes you see carry food from the yolk to the embryo.
See the baby snake's eyes and its coiled body?

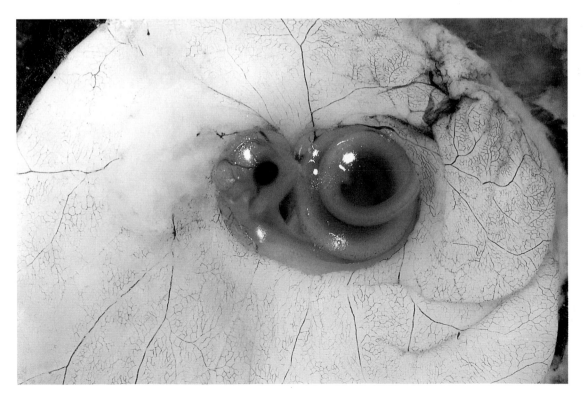

These hog-nosed snakes are just hatching. Different types of snakes develop faster than others. It may take from one to several months for a baby snake to be ready to hatch. Before the baby leaves the egg, it absorbs any remaining yolk into its body. Hopefully, this food supply will last long enough for the young snake to find its first meal. That may be a few weeks, months, or even a season later!

A baby snake has a small egg tooth at the front of its mouth. When the baby is ready to hatch, it moves its head from side to side to tear a slit in the tough eggshell with this tooth. Can you find an egg where the baby is just opening its shell? How many baby snakes are crawling out of their shells?

This baby hognose viper has just been born. Do you see a thin egg sac clinging to its lower body? In some snakes, the young grow inside the mother without a tough eggshell. When it is time for them to be born, the mother's muscles push the young snakes out of her body, one at a time.

These newborn baby snakes are with their mother now, but they will take care of themselves. Each little snake is already active. Within a couple of weeks, after shedding for the first time, the young snakes will begin to hunt for food and to grow. Clearly, snakes are special...from the inside out!

PRONUNCIATION GUIDE

CARBOHYDRATE   kär, - bō - hī′ - drāt,

CARBON DIOXIDE   kär′ - bən dī - äk′ - sīd,

EMBRYO   em′ - brē - ō,

MUSCLES   mə′ - səls

NUTRIENTS   nü′ - trē - ənts

OXYGEN   äk′ - si - jən

PROTEIN   prō′ - tēn,

SKELETON   ske′ - lə - tᵊn

VENOM   ve′ - nəm

VERTEBRAE   vər′- te - brā,

ä as in cart   ə as in banana   ü as in rule

*This beautiful snake is
called a rhinoceros viper.*

GLOSSARY/INDEX

ADDER: While there are different types of adders, the one in this book is a Peringuey's adder from South Africa's Namibian Desert. **12**

AFRICAN BUSH VIPER: This African snake most often lives in forests or swamps. **8**

AFRICAN EGG-EATING SNAKE: This slim-bodied snake found in Africa and Asia has a mouth and neck that can stretch to swallow eggs. **9**

ANAL SCALE: One big belly scale that marks where the snake's body stops and the tail begins **10**

BLACK RACER: One of a group of snakes most often found in the U.S. in grassy meadows **14**

BLACK RAT SNAKE: This U.S. snake is usually found in rocky places. **10**

BONES: The hard but lightweight parts that form a supporting frame for the snake's body **15-16, 26**

BRAIN: Body part that receives messages about what is happening inside and outside the body and that sends messages to put the body into action **22**

CANTIL: A Mexican snake related to the copperhead and the water moccasin **11-12**

CARBON DIOXIDE: Gas that is given off naturally in body activities, carried to the lungs by the blood, and breathed out **30, 33**

CELLS: Tiny building blocks for all body parts **13**

EMBRYO: Name given to the developing young **33**

EMERALD TREE BOA: This is a Central and South American rain forest snake. **8, 10**

FANG: A sharp tooth used to inject venom into the snake's prey **25**

GARTER SNAKE: A familiar snake of North America that can be found in fields or near ponds **22, 31**

HEART: Body part that acts like a pump, constantly pushing blood throughout the snake's body **30, 31**

HEAT-SENSITIVE PITS: Special groups of cells found in some snakes that make it possible for the snake to "spot" another animal **20**

HOG-NOSED SNAKES: Found in the U.S. and Mexico, these snakes have a hard, turned-up nose for burrowing. **34**

HOGNOSE VIPER: Most often found in Central and South America, this snake hunts mainly frogs and lizards. **24, 25, 35, 36**

KIDNEYS: Body part that removes wastes from blood **29**

LARGE INTESTINE: Tube where wastes are stored before leaving the body through the anal opening **29**

LUNG: Body part where oxygen and carbon dioxide are exchanged inside tiny, bubble-like air sacs **30**

MUSCLES: Working in pairs, muscles move the snake's bones by pulling on them. **16, 30, 35**

NUTRIENTS: Chemical building blocks into which food is broken down for use by the snake's body **28**

OXYGEN: A gas in the air that is breathed into the lungs, carried by the blood to the cells, and combined with food nutrients to release energy **30, 33**

PARROT SNAKE: This snake is found from southern Mexico through Central America to Argentina. **19**

PUPIL: Opening in the eye that lets light enter **19**

PYTHON: A group of snakes found in the tropics of Africa, Asia, and Australia **6, 7**

RATTLESNAKE: One of a group of snakes named for the noise its tail tip makes when shaken **20, 32**

SCALES: Places where the skin is thicker for extra protection **8, 9, 10**

SCENT-SENSITIVE PITS: Special groups of scent-sensitive cells in the roof of the snake's mouth **22**

SEA SNAKES: General name for all snakes living in the oceans **29**

SHEDDING: Peeling off the outer portion of dead skin, usually all in one piece **13, 14**

SKELETON: Framework of bones that supports the body and gives it its shape **15**

SKIN: Layers of cells that protect the snake's body and help keep it from drying out **8-14**

SMALL INTESTINE: The tube-shaped organ where food is mixed with special juices to break it down into nutrients **28**

STOMACH: Stretchy body part able to store and break down food before it enters the small intestine **28**

TROPICAL MILK SNAKE: One of a group of snakes noted for eating other snakes and rodents **23**

VENOM: Liquid poison produced in some snakes and injected through their bite to help them catch and begin breaking down food **25**

WINDPIPE: Tube through which air moves in and out of the snake's body **27**

YELLOW EYELASH VIPER: This rain forest snake is found in Mexico, Central America, and South America. **3, 4, 17, 18**

YOLK: Food supply for embryo while it develops **33, 34**

LOOKING BACK

1. As you discovered on page 14, snakes shed their skin to keep it from wearing out and to let them grow bigger. Imagine that you are a snake. How do you think it would feel to shed a body suit to grow bigger?

2. Snakes see everything from belly level. To find out what this is like, stand in the middle of your bedroom and look around. Next, stretch out on the floor and look around again. In what ways does your room look different from this snake's-eye view? Did you notice anything you didn't before?

3. Take another look at the snake trying to ambush the hummingbird on pages 17 and 18. Draw and color a third picture to show what you think happened next.

4. Do you remember how it helps a snake to be a long tube? (If not, look back on page 5.) What are some things you would miss being able to do if your body was a long tube?

5. Look back at the snake swallowing the frog on page 24. Did you notice that the snake is swallowing the frog headfirst? Can you guess why most snakes swallow their food headfirst? Here's a clue—picture an animal's arms and legs moving.

6. Make up a story about how the king snake on page 23 helped a farmer. Draw and color pictures to illustrate your story.

PHOTO CREDITS